CONTENTS

The Boy Who Stole the
PHARAOH'S LUNCH

KAREN McCOMBIE

Illustrated by
Anneli Bray

C334878500

For Catriona Keelan

First published in 2023 in Great Britain by
Barrington Stoke Ltd
18 Walker Street, Edinburgh, EH3 7LP

www.barringtonstoke.co.uk

Text © 2023 Karen McCombie
Illustrations © 2023 Anneli Bray

A CIP catalogue record for this book is available
from the British Library upon request

ISBN: 978-1-80090-201-5

Printed by Hussar Books, Poland

CHAPTER 1

The mummy mistake

Seth Davis was good at two things – gaming on his Xbox and being the class clown. He liked hanging out with his cat Muppet too, even if she was old and slept a lot. Everything else just made him feel bored.

Seth got bored at home when his parents made him get off his Xbox. He got bored when he had to play with his baby sister, Freema, because babies don't game.

And Seth got bored in school. He got fed up writing things out. He got fed up reading things in books and on the whiteboard.

This week Seth was very fed up with the topic his class was learning about – Ancient Egypt. He wanted to learn about cool stuff, like how the Ancient Egyptians made dead people into mummies. But his teacher Mr Ali went on and on about kings and queens and gods with really long names. The names were too hard to remember and too hard to spell!

In fact, everything about Ancient Egypt was hard to spell. Even the words "Ancient" and "Egypt" were hard to spell!

That morning Mr Ali had asked the class to draw a pyramid and then label things inside it. Mr Ali handed out the words for the things inside, like:

- antechamber

- amulet

- papyrus

- sarcophagus

- canopic jars

- hieroglyphics

But Seth got fed up with working out what the different words were. In the end he gave up and drew a scary mummy inside the pyramid. That was pretty funny!

Mr Ali *didn't* think it was funny and he told Seth he wanted to talk to him at break-time. Seth felt a bit worried about that. For just a minute. Then he got back to planning something else that was going to be very, very funny indeed!

*

In Assembly, Seth's class were giving a talk on what they'd learned about the Egyptians. Some pupils had been picked to do the talking and explaining part. The rest of the class were standing at the back of the hall and they were going to sing an old pop song called "Walk Like an Egyptian".

Mr Ali didn't see that Seth had snuck away.

No one spotted that he had gone to the boys' toilet and changed into a costume that he got for a Halloween party last year. It was a mummy costume, with a mask like a skull!

And now Seth was at the hall door, looking inside and grinning to himself. He'd had to take off his glasses because of the mask, so things were a bit fuzzy. But Seth could tell that the hall of Weston Primary School was packed.

Seth was ready. This was it!

He ran into the hall and gave a scary roar. Bits of white cloth flapped from his arms. He heard shouts and laughing.

Everyone loved Seth's joke!

But then he heard a sound that made him worried. Seth looked down at the rows of

pupils at the front of the hall. A small boy was sobbing hard. And he wasn't the only one. Lots of the little children were crying now!

Was this mummy idea a mistake?

"Seth Davis!" Mr Ali yelled. "Get out NOW and wait for me back in class!"

Uh-oh ...

CHAPTER 2

From here to where?

It was break-time but Seth was inside, waiting in the classroom for Mr Ali to come and tell him off. He heard sounds of chatting and giggling from the playground outside.

It was hard for Seth to sit still. The mummy costume was hot but the zip at the back was stuck. Seth took off the mask but he was still too hot.

Seth put his glasses back on. He tapped the toes of his new red trainers on the floor. He drummed his fingers on Mr Ali's table.

Then Seth spotted something small but interesting next to Mr Ali's laptop. It was a beetle. A shiny golden beetle made of metal. Seth remembered that the Ancient Egyptians loved this kind of beetle because it meant happiness or good luck or something.

Seth picked up the beetle. It felt cool in his hand. He closed his eyes and tried to remember what this type of beetle was called. It had a special name.

*

Seth felt a shiver of cold. From his waist down he was suddenly very chilly.

Seth opened his eyes. He looked from side to side. He was not in the classroom and he was not sitting on a blue plastic chair any more.

Seth was standing in greeny-brown water that came up to his belly button! Where was he? Was he in a pond or a lake? How had he got here?

All around Seth were thick grassy reeds. He didn't know what was behind them. But there was something coming *towards* him!

Seth saw the tall reeds begin to move. He heard a swooshing sound getting closer and closer.

All of a sudden a huge head loomed out at him …

"Aaah!" yelled Seth.

The head didn't belong to Mr Ali. It was a giant cow with horns and floppy ears. The cow was standing next to Seth in the water and it was enormous. It looked as if it could trample Seth very easily!

But the giant cow didn't seem to want to trample Seth. It stared at him with huge dark eyes as if it was trying to work out what Seth was doing and why. Seth wished he knew himself.

And now there were *more* swooshing sounds.

Another animal bounced out of the reeds. This one looked like a dog. It had a crazy tuft of hair in between its fluffy, round ears.

"Uh ... there's a good boy!" said Seth,
copying the way his aunty spoke to her dog –
a yappy cockapoo called Peanut.

The dog didn't wag its tail like Peanut did.
It opened its mouth and it had very sharp teeth.

"Help!" yelled Seth. "Please, someone, help me!"

Then the animal made a very odd sound. It was not a bark or a growl or a snarl.

It was a giggle. A squeaky high giggle!

Was the weird dog laughing at him?

It didn't matter. There was another swoosh in the reeds and Seth saw a girl looking down at him.

And she was not alone.

CHAPTER 3

Far away and long ago

"Who are you?" the girl asked.

She looked about the same age as Seth. There was a small boy peeking out from behind her legs. The girl wore a sort of floppy white dress and her dark hair was tied into lots of thick, stubby braids. The little boy had no clothes on at all and he was almost bald.

"Who are YOU?" Seth asked back, trying to be brave.

"I'm Mery," the girl said. "This is my brother, Pash. We live here, and you don't." She gave the giant cow a big bash on the neck. It slowly turned and went away. The weird-looking giggling dog didn't go anywhere. It stayed by the girl's side.

"Where is *here*?" Seth asked.

"Amarna," said Mery. "Where are *you* from?"

Seth said nothing – his head was spinning. He didn't remember a village or town called Amarna near where he lived.

Mery looked at him again.

"Are you unwell?" she asked. "Did you fall from a boat? Or jump?"

Seth didn't know what to say. He didn't know what was going on. And until he did, he thought he wouldn't say anything.

"A young slave jumped into the river near here last year," said Mery.

"A slave?" said Seth, shocked. What was going on? What sort of place had slaves? No one in Weston was a slave!

"Some fishermen helped the slave," Mery carried on. "He said he was running away from an evil master. Do you have an evil master?"

"Not really," said Seth. Mr Ali got cross with him when he was being silly, but he was a teacher, not a master. And Mr Ali was sometimes a bit bossy but never evil.

"What happened to the slave boy?" Seth asked.

"Oh, he died," said Mery. "He was bitten by a crocodile before the fishermen pulled him out of the river. My mother tried to help him get better but he didn't live long."

"A CROCODILE?!" Seth shouted. He looked around him so fast he made waves in the water. "There are crocodiles here?"

"Of course there are crocodiles in the Nile!" said Mery, holding her hand out to him. "And hippos. And snakes."

Seth didn't want to stay in the water for one more second. He grabbed Mery's hand and jumped out of the water and up onto the bank beside her.

Seth stood, his legs shaking, and heard a giggle, but it was not the weird dog this time. Mery's little brother, Pash, was pointing at what Seth was wearing.

Seth looked down at himself and saw that the top half of the mummy costume was ripped off. His chest was bare. Where was his school polo shirt? At least the mummy outfit was still on his bottom half. And he was still wearing his new trainers and socks, even if they were very muddy and wet.

"Come on," said Mery as she turned and pushed past the reeds. "I may need to shoo the water buffalo away from the crops."

Was Mery talking about the cow that had been in the water beside Seth? Was it actually a water buffalo? Seth felt more puzzled than ever.

But there was no time to think because Mery and her brother were walking away.

Seth saw that Pash was holding on to the neck hair of the giggling dog.

"What kind of dog is that?" Seth asked as he ran after all three of them.

"Don't you know what a hyena is?" said Mery, looking back at him. "Don't you have them where you come from?"

Seth didn't answer. They had pushed past the tall reeds and what he saw now was even more of a surprise. There were lots of green fields with crops and small trees. And beyond them was a village with red stone walls and houses.

And in the distance Seth saw something that made him gasp. It was a huge palace with tall pillars and towering stone statues. It was just the sort of palace a Pharaoh would live in.

Suddenly Seth understood.

There was a Pharaoh's palace. The River Nile. Water buffalo and hyenas. Crocodiles, hippos, snakes and slaves.

Seth Davis wasn't in Weston Primary School any more, and he wasn't in his own time.

Seth was somewhere very, very far away, and in a time very, very long ago. He held on tight to the golden beetle he had picked up from Mr Ali's table.

"How did this happen?" he whispered to himself as he followed Mery, Pash and the hyena across the dry earth of Ancient Egypt ...

CHAPTER 4

The wrong name

Seth's heart beat fast as he looked at the grand palace and the red desert behind it.

"Does King Tutankhamun live there?" Seth asked as he walked with Mery and Pash.

King Tutankhamun was the most famous Pharaoh of them all. He was also the only one Seth could remember Mr Ali talking about.

Mery turned to stare at Seth. Then she burst out laughing.

"The holy Pharaoh Akhenaten is king!" she said. "His son Tutankhamun is just a tiny child.

Younger than my brother. How can you not know this?"

"Sorry, I got muddled up," said Seth. "What about the pyramids? Are they near here? Are they being built right now?"

"The pyramids? They are many days north of here," said Mery. "And no, they are not being built right now – the pyramids are more than 1,000 years old!"

Seth's head was spinning. So the pyramids were ancient even to Ancient Egyptians like Mery? How long did the Ancient Egyptian times go on for? Seth wished he'd listened to what Mr Ali had told them in class ...

"I think your head is full of river water," said Mery. "I'll take you home to Mother. She knows about medicine and will get you well again."

Seth felt like his head was melting. Had he really gone back in time? But how? Or was he just having some sort of dream?

He looked at the people working in the fields. There were men and boys with donkeys and water buffalo to help them pull things along. Women and children picked fruit from the trees and filled baskets. They all looked pretty real to Seth ...

"I'm going to get Mother!" Pash shouted as they got into the village. He ran off towards one of the houses. The hyena looked up at Mery as if it was waiting for her. It made the weird laughing sound Seth had heard when he was stuck in the river.

"Giggler, go!" said Mery, and pointed at the hyena to follow her brother.

"It's called Giggler? Because of the noise it makes?" asked Seth as the hyena galloped after the boy.

"Yes," said Mery. "He came to our yard when he was very young. He was starving and rooting around for food. I asked Mother and Father if I could keep him, and they said yes. It's my job to feed him scraps – to make him grow fat and strong."

As they talked, Seth saw that the village was made up of small square houses that looked like sheds made of dried red mud. Each house had a circle of wall around it to make a yard. Up ahead, Seth saw Pash and Giggler vanish behind a wall. It was time to see Mery's home.

Seth looked around the yard. The ground was just dusty earth. A big grey goose honked at him and flapped its wide wings. There were pots of different shapes and sizes stacked up on the ground. There were stone steps at the side of the house that led up to the flat roof.

Seth stared, but he wasn't the only one.

In the door stood a woman in a white cloth dress like Mery's.

"So this is the poor boy!" the woman said, and came quickly towards him. She kicked Giggler out of the way.

Suddenly Mery's mum had her hands on the sides of Seth's head.

"Is this some sort of amulet that your people wear?" she asked, looking at his glasses.

Seth couldn't remember what an amulet was. He just nodded and hoped that would do.

"Open your eyes wide, boy!" Mery's mum said.

Seth did as he was told.

"Now open your mouth!"

Seth felt the woman's fingers go into his mouth, pulling his cheeks this way and that. What was she looking for in there?

"Your eyes and gums are a good colour. You are healthy," Mery's mum told him as she let go of him. "But you can't think clearly?"

Seth shook his head. He didn't know how to tell her what he felt.

"Come, come," said Mery's mum. "Have some food, boy. That will make you feel better. And I'll say a prayer to Aken for you."

Who is "Aken"? Seth thought. But Pash had grabbed what was left of Seth's mummy costume and was pulling him into the house.

Mery's home felt dark after the bright sunlight outside.

"Is this the lad that nearly drowned and doesn't know where he is?" said a man sitting cross-legged on the floor. Next to him was an older teenage boy. They both had shaved heads and bare feet. It looked like they were wearing white kilts. "Do you know your name at least?" the man asked.

"Seth," said Seth.

There were gasps around the room.

Seth looked over at Mery. Had he said something wrong?

"Never say that name in my house again!" the man shouted at him. "Do you hear me? NEVER!"

Seth was shocked. Sometimes his parents or his teacher got a bit cross with him when he was silly, but no one had ever been this angry with him before.

"Father, he is not well! He doesn't understand!" Mery shouted.

"Here's what he needs to understand," the man said. "If the Pharaoh hears that name, we are all in danger. And YOU most of all, boy!"

Seth saw how angry the man was. He looked scared too. Seth began to panic. More than anything he wanted to turn and run away, to run back home. But how was he going to get home when he didn't understand how he got here or where to go?

Seth's head felt dizzy, his knees went soft and he started to shake. The golden beetle fell from his hand as he slumped to the ground. The last thing he saw was a scorpion scurry past his nose, then everything went black.

CHAPTER 5

Lucky charms

Seth woke up because his face was being licked.

"Stop it, Freema!" he said. His little sister was always doing yucky things like trying to lick or bite him or even kiss him. Mum and Dad thought it was funny. Seth thought it was disgusting. Babies were so gross!

Or maybe it was Muppet the cat, sneaking into Seth's room and curling up for a snooze on his pillow.

But when Seth opened his eyes, Freema wasn't there. Muppet wasn't there. Seth's bedroom with the Superman curtains wasn't there. Seth was looking right up at a pinky dawn sky. He was sleeping on a mat on the flat roof of the red mud house. Giggler sat by his side, ready to lick him some more.

"Go away, Giggler!" Mery told the hyena. He slunk off and sat down.

Seth tried not to cry. He was still stuck in Ancient Egypt, far from home. Then he thought of the angry faces from the night before.

"What happened?" asked Seth as he sat up and grabbed his glasses. "How did I get here?"

He looked around – there were more mats laid out on the roof but no one else was sleeping on them. Pash was playing with a wooden toy mouse. He was pulling a string that made the tail move.

"You passed out," said Mery. "My father and brother carried you up here. You have slept for many hours."

"I saw a scorpion!" Seth remembered. "Did it bite me?"

"It didn't bite you!" Mery said happily. "You'd be dead if it had. My big brother Neheb killed the scorpion with a stone."

Seth was glad. Yes, the scorpion had died but he hadn't. Then he remembered how angry Mery's dad and brother Neheb had been.

"What did I say that made everyone so upset?" Seth asked.

"You told us your name was ..." Mery began to whisper. She mouthed "Seth" at him.

"What's wrong with that?" asked Seth.

"That's the name of the god of mischief!" Mery told him.

"Cool!" Seth said with a grin. Class clown, god of mischief. He'd like a T-shirt with that printed on it when he got back to his own time!

Mery didn't understand why Seth was grinning.

"It isn't funny!" she snapped. "You can't say that name out loud. You can't talk about *any* of the old gods!"

Seth suddenly remembered the names of some of the gods Mr Ali had put on the whiteboard.

"Hey, Anubis is the god that looks like a dog," said Seth. "Right? He's the god of death!" He was getting excited. "And Ra – that's easy to spell. That's the sun god. And—"

Mery slapped a hand over Seth's mouth to shut him up.

"All the old gods are banned! How can you not know this?" Mery hissed at him.

"Um, maybe because of the accident? In the river?" said Seth as he pushed Mery's hand away.

Mery nodded as if what he said made sense.

"The Pharaoh will only let us worship *one* god now," Mery said. "That is Aten, the true sun god."

Aten ... Mery's mum had told Seth she was going to say a prayer to Aten before he passed out.

Now he saw that Mery was holding up a necklace. It was a small, flat piece of stone tied on to a thin piece of leather.

"This is Aten," said Mery.

Seth stared at the stone – something was carved on it. It was a sun with rays coming from it. And at the end of each ray were funny-looking hands! Seth almost giggled but thought he'd better not.

So he pointed to something tied to the end of one of Mery's braids. It was a tiny stone fish.

"Why do you have a fish in your hair?" Seth asked her.

"To protect me from drowning, of course!" said Mery. "And Pash has an amulet to keep him safe from harm."

Pash heard his name and came nearer. He held up a tiny bag that was on a string around his neck.

"What's in there? Lots of little stone fish?" Seth asked with a smile.

"No, silly!" said Pash. "Mouse bones. Real ones!"

Pash spilled tiny bones out of the bag and into his own hand. Seth stared at them. He had remembered amulets were lucky charms but these stone fish and real mouse bones were so strange!

"You have amulets too," said Mery. She pointed at Seth's glasses and then at his arm. "You dropped this scarab beetle when you fainted. Mother tied it on for you."

Seth looked down. A piece of the mummy bandage was wrapped around his wrist. There was a bump in it where Mr Ali's golden beetle must be.

The beetle ...

For a few seconds Seth forgot to take a breath. He had just worked something out. He had been holding Mr Ali's beetle when he got transported back in time. The beetle had to have something to do with Seth being here in Ancient Egypt! And if that was true, then surely it could help him get back home? Home to Weston Primary School. Home to Mum, Dad, his sister Freema and Muppet the cat.

Seth just had to work out how …

"Hungry?" Mery asked.

Yes, he was! Lucky charms and solving time-travel problems would have to wait. Seth's tummy was rumbling, whatever part of history he was stuck in.

CHAPTER 6

Hard work and good news

In the last half an hour, Seth had found out three surprising things about life in Ancient Egypt:

1. Food was not like at home. He had never eaten grapes, fish and onions for breakfast.

2. Children were expected to brush their teeth – using twigs.

3. Toilets were stools with holes in them that were put over boxes of sand outside the back of the house. Just like a cat's litter box!

And now Seth had his very own white linen kilt to wear. It was one of Mery's big brother's. The kilt looked kind of cool with Seth's red trainers!

"Your shoes are so odd ..." said Mery as they walked out of the yard of her house. The grumpy goose honked after them.

Seth saw that Mery's feet were bare. He didn't know how she could walk on the baking-hot earth.

"They're pretty normal where I come from," Seth told her. Lots of the kids in his class had the same trainers, all in different colours.

"Where is that? Can you remember now?" Mery asked, looking hopeful.

"Um, no," said Seth. How could he even start to tell her about the playground at Weston with everyone running around playing tag? He bet children here never had fun. He didn't know what life was like for the rich kids, like the Pharaoh's children. But Seth could see that ordinary kids in the village had to help their parents with their work all day long. Even little ones like Pash.

"We'll go to the trees and pick dates with Mother soon," said Mery. "But first I'll show you around the village. Most of the older boys have left home to work at the palace. So the men will be happy to give a strong boy like you a job!"

Seth felt odd. He was only a kid and in school. How could he have a job? But then it was kind of cool to think he was strong and could be useful. He'd never felt useful before.

"And I have a new name for you," said Mery. "We will tell everyone that you are called Idu. It means 'Boy'!"

"Idu! Idu!" said Pash, skipping beside them and grabbing hold of Seth's hand. Giggler trotted along too, like a pet dog.

*

The first person Seth met was the potter.

"Everyone needs pots and bowls," said the potter, sitting Seth down on a bench nearby. "Here, Idu, have a try!"

Seth ran his hands over the wet clay of a tall pot that was going to be used for collecting water. Seth made a handle for it and the potter was pleased.

The second person Seth met was a man who turned reeds and papyrus leaves into baskets and fishing nets. Seth had a go at that too, and it was fun weaving the pieces together like a puzzle.

Next Seth met a farmer. The farmer talked about his donkey and how to look after it. He even explained how he sang to the donkey in the fields to make it happy and work harder.

The farmer spoke about how important the weather was to grow his crops. He told Seth that the Nile flooded every year and covered the fields but that was good for the soil.

Mery pointed out the fishermen on their boats in the Nile.

"You can meet the fishermen tonight when they come back," she said. "Maybe you can try going out on the river with them tomorrow?"

"Maybe," said Seth. The truth was that Seth hoped that he'd be back in Weston by tomorrow and not in Egypt any more. That he'd be sitting in class with his friends, listening to Mr Ali talking. He never thought he'd miss his teacher so much!

"There's the palace too," said Mery. "You could work there. Can you read and write?"

"Like hieroglyphics?" asked Seth. He knew a few of the Egyptian letters that Mr Ali had shown the class. A snake was the letter "J". An owl was the letter "M".

"They always need scribes to write down prayers and laws and things," said Mery. "You only need to know a little. They would train you."

Seth shook his head as he looked towards the Pharaoh's palace in the distance.

"I'm not that good at reading and writing," he told her.

Seth wasn't talking about hieroglyphics now. He was talking about the reading and writing he did at school. He found it really hard. The words kept moving and changing shape. He'd never told anyone before. Not his parents, not his teachers. This was the first time he'd said anything about it.

"Well, let's see how good you are at picking dates!" said Mery. They'd got to the trees where Mery's mum and others were hard at work. The dates hung in bunches under the branches.

Seth looked up at the fruit. He had never even tasted a date, never mind picked one!

Mery handed him one out of a basket. "They taste of toffee!" Seth told her.

"I don't know what toffee is!" Mery said with a laugh.

*

The time passed quickly. Seth was keen to show how many baskets he could fill and how high he could climb to get dates in the treetops.

"You're a good boy, Idu," said Mery's
mum when they stopped to eat. "You're a
hard worker."

Seth ripped his bread in two and poured olive oil over it. He was so hungry that it tasted as good as a pizza. He shared some with Giggler, who pushed at Seth's leg with his nose, looking for scraps.

"All the men were pleased with Idu too," Mery told her mum.

"That's good," Mery's mum said, nodding. "You can have a good life in the village, Idu."

Seth smiled at her but inside he suddenly felt panic again. He didn't want to have a good life in the village. He already had a good life, with his family and his friends. He wanted to get back home to them and soon!

And then he heard shouting. Everyone turned to see what was happening. Mery's brother Neheb was running towards them all. He worked as a baker with Mery's father and he had brown flour dust all over his hands and his arms and his face.

"I have news!" Neheb shouted. "The Pharaoh and his people are coming here tomorrow. To the river!"

Everyone began talking at once. They all looked excited. Everyone talked of gifts they'd give to the Pharaoh when he came to visit. It was a big deal for the Pharaoh to leave his palace and visit the river, Seth could tell.

"It will be a great day! Full of prayers, full of marvels!" Mery's mum said.

Full of marvels? Perhaps it would be a lucky day for Seth too. The day when he got back to where he belonged. The day the beetle worked its magic again. But first he wanted to see a real, live, famous Pharaoh!

CHAPTER 7

Time to play!

The grown-ups got together to talk about how they would welcome the Pharaoh. They didn't mind all the children going off to have fun!

"Come on!" said Mery, pulling Seth by the arm so they could join the other kids.

They played game after game.

The first one was the Star game, where one boy stood with his arms out. Two children grabbed each of his hands. Other kids grabbed *their* hands. The boy in the middle spun around, along with all the others.

The spinning got faster and faster till the people at the end of the "star" shape went flying into the dirt.

Everyone was laughing, including Giggler the hyena!

Next they played a piggyback ball game. Children sat up on each other's backs and threw a ball made of leaves to each other.

"Hey, let's play piggyback in the river!" someone shouted.

Everyone ran and jumped into the Nile. Seth stayed at the edge.

"Come on, Idu!" Mery called out to him. Even Pash was swimming and splashing about like a baby seal.

Seth loved swimming at home. But there were no crocodiles and hippos and snakes in the local pool in Weston.

"Is it safe?" said Seth.

"It's fine!" one of the older boys told him. "There's nothing around. Come in – or are you too scared?"

Seth normally loved playing in the water. But something didn't feel right. Even Giggler was acting oddly.

The hyena stood by Seth's side and its ha-ha-ha noise sounded more like a panic sort of sound than a giggle.

"What is it, Giggler?" Seth asked. He looked out across the wide, wide Nile. There was nothing to see except a floating log.

But then Giggler started to howl and Seth saw that the log was moving. Moving way too fast. The log was moving like a long dart towards the children who were splashing and playing.

"CROCODILE!" shouted Seth. "Get out of the water!"

The splashing and playing was replaced by shouts and screams. Everyone swam for the riverbank. Some people were already pulling themselves up onto dry land and safety.

But now Seth saw that Mery was not a strong swimmer. Was that why she had a fish amulet tied in her hair?

Mery was trying to grab Pash, but her little brother kept bobbing out of reach.

Seth had his Level 7 certificate from swimming lessons back home. He could do this.

"Mery – get out!" he yelled.

Seth dived as fast and far into the river as he could. As soon as his head came above water, he saw he was right beside Pash.

"Get on my back! Hold tight!" Seth told Pash. Then Seth swam for his life – and Pash's. He didn't look back.

Seth saw how scared everyone on the riverbank looked. They had pulled Mery out of the water and were shouting, "Idu! Idu, hurry!"

Lots of children held their arms out to him. Seth felt their fingers dig in to his skin as they

grabbed him, pulling Seth and Pash up onto the bank. Even Giggler tugged at Seth's wet kilt to get him out.

"Run, Idu!" someone called out. "The crocodile could come up out of the water after us!"

And so Seth ran, holding Pash in his arms.

His head pounded and his chest burned like it was on fire. But Seth had never been more proud of himself!

CHAPTER 8

The Pharaoh's lunch

The next morning, once again Seth was licked awake by a hyena instead of being woken by his mum banging at his bedroom door.

Seth's hand curled around the bit of cloth that held the golden beetle. It had let him down again. Would he ever work out how to get home?

"Good morning, sleepy-head!" said Mery, sitting by his mat. Pash was there too, playing with his wooden toy mouse. The little boy seemed pretty happy for someone who had nearly been a crocodile's supper!

Mery's family had been so happy that Seth had kept Pash safe. They had made him a special meal. A dinner for a hero.

The meat they had cooked smelled and tasted great. And Mery's mum had used herbs and spices on it that the Weston Primary School cook never put on the burgers that Seth had for lunch every Friday.

Seth had been made to feel very welcome. Much more welcome than the day before, when Mery's family had been so angry with him.

"Morning ..." said Seth now as he felt around for his glasses.

He yawned. He needed to brush his teeth. The "beer" that everyone drank around here had given Seth bad breath. But he'd have to watch out for splinters with that stick toothbrush – he'd nearly got one in his gum the day before.

"There's lots to do today," Mery said as she jumped to her feet. "Come on!"

Seth was still sleepy and had to go slowly down the steps at the side of the house. Pash and Giggler both got in his way. They were both laughing at him, just as excited as Mery.

"I can't wait to see the great Pharaoh Akhenaten!" said Mery. She was dancing around in the yard.

Seth looked around for the grumpy goose. *All the dancing and chatter must have made that goose fly off*, he thought. Any second now it would come back and honk at them to shut up.

"And little Prince Tutankhamun ..." said Mery. "Do you think he will wear gold and jewels even if he is just a baby?"

"Maybe," said Seth.

But he wasn't thinking about gold and jewels and babies. Seth had suddenly remembered some stuff about Tutankhamun. Mr Ali had shown the class a video about him. He became Pharaoh when he was just a boy about the same age as Seth.

And then Seth remembered even more stuff from the video. Experts in Ancient Egypt had found out that King Tutankhamun had only been a teenager when he'd died. He'd been buried in a fancy tomb in a place called the Valley of the Kings.

King Tutankhamun's mummified body had stayed hidden there for over 3,000 years. Then it'd been discovered in 1922 along with all the treasure that had been buried with him.

Seth frowned. He used to think mummies were funny but now it seemed pretty sad and strange to dig up someone's body and put all their stuff on show.

But one thing was for sure – Seth wasn't going to tell Mery about any of that. It would be too hard for her to hear. And she'd probably think he was making it up!

"Where's your silly goose?" Seth asked.

He patted down the spiky tuft of hair between Giggler's ears. The hyena was just as much of a hero as Seth was. After all, it had seen the crocodile first. Seth was glad that Mery's family had given the hyena just as much meat as they gave him last night. Giggler deserved it!

"The goose?" said Mery as she stopped dancing and spinning. "You ate it yesterday! Father killed it for your feast!"

"What?" said Seth. He felt as if someone had punched him in the chest. Of course he knew that meat came from animals. But he'd never got to know an animal before he'd eaten it before!

"Didn't you like the meat?" Mery asked.

"Yes ... yes, but ..."

Seth didn't know how to explain. Of course it was normal for Mery and her friends to grow their own food and eat animals that lived with them in their village. It was just a bit of a shock for him, that was all.

"The meal was great. Thank you," said Seth as he remembered his manners. Mery and her family had looked after him. They'd let him stay in their house with them. Until Seth could get home, he wanted to show them he was brave and hard-working.

"Well, come on! Help me find wood for a really big fire!" said Mery.

She hurried out of the yard. Seth ran after her with Pash and Giggler.

"Why do we need a really big fire?" Seth asked.

"Because our family needs to cook something special for the Pharaoh," Mery said.

"What are you going to cook?" said Seth. It was fun to learn what a Pharaoh would have for his picnic by the river!

But Seth didn't like the answer one bit.

"Giggler, of course!" said Mery. "I've been fattening him up for a special feast like this!"

Seth stopped so fast he nearly fell over. Giggler came running over to him, just to check he was all right.

The hyena licked his hand and Seth found it hard not to cry.

Giggler was going to be the Pharaoh's lunch?

CHAPTER 9

Ready to run

The yard was busy, with everyone running around. Neheb was throwing more wood on the fire. Mery and her mother were grinding spices. Mery's father was busy baking bread to go with the meat they would cook for the Pharaoh. Pash was singing and skipping around.

Seth snuck away to the flat roof to think.

From up here, he could see the palace in the distance. The doors were open and a long line of people and wagons were beginning to leave and head this way.

Seth also saw that every house in the village was as busy as Mery's. Smoke drifted up from cooking fires. Voices drifted up too, sounding excited. Mery had told Seth that families were hoping to see their sons who had gone to work at the palace as servants and scribes and soldiers.

The only person in the village who wasn't happy was Seth. He rubbed at the bandage that Mery's mother had tied to his wrist and felt the hard round shape of the beetle underneath.

"Please, please take me away from here. Please take me home," Seth said softly.

Nothing happened. Now what? If he was stuck here, there *was* something good that Seth could do.

Something that would *not* make him a hero to Mery's family.

Something that would make him an enemy.

Seth looked down at the hyena. Giggler was lying sleeping just outside the yard walls. Before he could chicken out, Seth ran down the stairs at the side of the house. No one saw him slip inside, looking for leftover scraps of food.

"Yes!" he said to himself as he grabbed a bit of goose meat from a bowl.

"I'll get more sticks for the fire!" Seth called out as he ran out of the house past everyone.

"We don't need any more!" Neheb shouted, but Seth was already gone.

"Here!" Seth hissed at the sleepy hyena.

Giggler's nose sniffed at the meat. He got up.

"Come on!" Seth called to Giggler. He ran as fast as he could and Giggler galloped by

Seth's side happily. His nose kept sniffing for the treat Seth held in his hand.

Seth's plan was to get Giggler far away from the village and the Pharaoh who was coming to visit. Seth would keep running along the riverbank in the opposite direction until the Pharaoh and his people had gone away.

It meant that Seth wouldn't see the famous King Tutankhamun but that wasn't as important as stopping Giggler from being eaten.

After that, Seth had no plan. If he went back to Mery's house, her family would be angry with him. Maybe they would tell him to leave. Maybe they would beat him! But Seth didn't care. Keeping Giggler safe was all that mattered.

But where was Giggler?

Seth slowed down. The hyena wasn't next to him any more. Seth looked around and saw Giggler running off towards some bushes. What was there? What had the hyena spotted?

Seth stopped. He tried to catch his breath. He saw something move around the bushes. He heard a chatter of giggles. It looked like Giggler had come across a pack of wild hyenas!

"Giggler!" Seth called out, with his arms in the air.

He worried that the wild pack would snarl or scare the tame hyena away.

"Giggler!" Seth called again.

But the hyena took no notice. It was with the pack. Seth saw the animals sniff at each other. And then there was a sharp noise, like a trumpet coming from the distant palace. The animals shot off together. Giggler was with them. Giggler had found a family! Would

he be safe now? Seth hoped so. He let his arms drop. He felt something fall.

Seth looked down and saw the bandage hanging from his wrist. The cloth had come loose. The scarab beetle had fallen and was rolling towards the river's edge.

"No!" yelled Seth as he ran after the metal insect and saw it plop into the Nile.

Seth felt sick. The golden charm was his only chance of escape. Was he now stuck in the past for ever?

Then Seth saw something glint in a clump of reeds. The beetle! It was risky but he knew he had to get it back. He'd be in and out of the river in a flash – before any crocodiles spotted him!

Seth splashed into the river and grabbed the beetle. He held it tight in his fist to keep it safe. But as he turned to get out, his trainers slipped. Seth slid deeper and deeper into the slippery mud. He tried to swim but the weeds around his ankles pulled him down, down, down …

As his head went under the water, the last thing Seth saw was the blue sky and the yellow reeds.

Seth started to choke. He was going to drown, if a crocodile didn't get to him first! Then everything went dark.

*

"Seth?" said a voice. "Seth? Are you OK? Or is this another one of your jokes?"

Seth began to blink. He opened his eyes and saw Mr Ali staring at him.

CHAPTER 10

Back to now

"I'm OK. I think," Seth said to his teacher.

Seth's head was spinning. His heart was thudding. But how could he explain to Mr Ali what had just happened? Seth didn't understand himself. Was any of it even real?

Seth looked down at the mummy costume. It was dry and it wasn't ripped. The mask he'd worn at Assembly was still in his lap.

"What have you got there?" asked Mr Ali. He sat on the edge of his desk and pointed at Seth's hand.

Seth looked down. The golden beetle sat in the middle of his hand.

The golden beetle that had taken Seth far, far away, far back in time, and then returned him here.

"This is very special, sir," said Seth. "Where did you get it?"

The beetle had to be treasure. It had to be very ancient. It had to be magical.

"This?" said Mr Ali, picking the shiny insect out of Seth's hand. "I got it from a market stall when I went to Egypt on holiday a few years ago. It was just there with lots of stuff for tourists to buy."

Seth blinked at Mr Ali. Only a few minutes had passed in the classroom – it was still break-time. Seth could hear the voices outside in the playground. But he'd been in Ancient

Egypt with Mery and her family for two whole days.

He'd had fun playing with other children. He'd loved finding out about the jobs he could do and how well he could do them. He'd been braver than he thought he could ever be and saved Pash and Giggler. He'd been so much more than the class clown, or the rubbish brother who got grumpy with Freema and who stayed shut up in his bedroom with his Xbox and a snoozy cat all the time …

Was all of that really just a dream?

"So, let's get back to this morning," Mr Ali said sternly. "Do you have anything to say for yourself, Seth?"

Mr Ali was talking about Seth's mummy stunt in Assembly. But Seth suddenly had something to say – something important. Something he should have told Mr Ali a long time ago.

"Mr Ali, I find stuff hard in class," said Seth.

Mr Ali's face changed.

"What sort of stuff?" asked Mr Ali. He was frowning at Seth but not in a cross or grumpy way.

"I don't find reading very easy. And writing is tricky too," said Seth. It felt scary but good to say out loud.

"I thought it looked like some things were tricky for you," said Mr Ali. "That explains why you don't always concentrate in class. And why you can act a bit silly!"

The bell rang loudly and made them both jump.

"Look, go and sit down and we can talk more about this later. OK?" Mr Ali said with a kind smile.

"OK," said Seth.

"I'm really glad you've told me that, Seth," Mr Ali went on. "It means we can look at ways to help you for sure!"

There was lots of noise in the corridor as Seth's classmates came back from break.

Seth got up from Mr Ali's desk and went to go to his own table. But something felt strange. And wet.

Seth looked down at his red trainers.

They were soaked, with reeds and mud stuck to them.

Seth smiled as he walked across the carpet tiles, leaving a trail of wet Nile footprints behind him ...

The facts behind the story ...

Ordinary people's lives

When we look at history, we always find out about how the rich and powerful people lived. And with Ancient Egypt, it's the kings and queens and their palaces and tombs that are talked about. Plus the yucky facts about mummies! But it's even more fun to find out how normal children lived, and that's why I chose to set Seth's story in Mery's village.

How long did the Ancient Egyptian period last?

When Seth finds himself in Ancient Egypt, he asks Mery if the pyramids are being built. He's shocked when she says that they were built more than 1,000 years before. That gives you an idea of how long that period was – Ancient Egyptian civilisation lasted about 3,000 years, and that time was split into the Old Kingdom, the Middle Kingdom and the New Kingdom. Mery lived in the time of the New Kingdom.

Why was Pharaoh Akhenaten important?

When people think of Ancient Egypt, they might think of all the gods the Egyptians believed in, like Ra or Anubis. But when King Akhenaten came to power, he banned people from worshipping all these gods. He decided there was only one true god – Aten, the sun-god. King Akhenaten's people must have found this difficult and confusing.

Akhenaten is also important because he was the father of the most famous Pharaoh of all – the boy king Tutankhamun. King Tutankhamun was only nine when he became ruler of Egypt and the first thing he did was allow people to worship all the old gods again.

Amulets

As Seth remembered, amulets are charms that people wear to keep them safe from harm or bring them luck.

Scarab beetles were popular as amulets in Ancient Egypt. The people thought they represented the circle of life – birth, life, death and re-birth. That sounds very grand for a small insect, and especially for one that's known by a different name – a dung beetle. Yes, dung means poo!

Medicine

Plants, herbs, honey and salt were used by Ancient Egyptians to help heal where they were hurt and cure illnesses. It makes sense because we know that honey is anti-bacterial, for example. Ancient Egyptians also performed surgery and made things like wooden toes for people who had lost part of their feet.

But when they couldn't find a cure for things, they did try prayers and even spells.

Just like us?

As you've seen from Seth's story, children in Ancient Egypt had things in common with kids today. They played games together, such as the Star game that Seth joined in with, and football, using a ball made of tightly bound papyrus leaves.

And yes, Ancient Egyptian children had to brush their teeth using small sticks. Toothpaste was made from things like ashes, burnt eggshells and salt. I bet you won't complain about minty toothpaste now!

Dyslexia

At the end of this story, Seth tells Mr Ali that he finds reading and writing quite hard. Mr Ali might be thinking that perhaps Seth has dyslexia. The good news is that dyslexia has nothing to do with how smart a person is! It's about how the brain tries to make sense of written words and sounds.

Sometimes teachers and carers can see that a child has dyslexia. But sometimes it can be harder to spot, with a young person getting very tired with all the extra effort they need to make in class. Or they can be like Seth, being silly or finding another way to take the attention away from how hard they are finding some of what they have to do at school. But with the right help, reading and writing can become a lot easier.